Stories for

for

Year Olds

Stories
for

Year Olds

Mandy Archer
Gabi Murphy

bookoli

Contents

Splish! Splash! Splosh! 6

Peekaboo Pup 12

Can't Catch Me! 20

Tickle Time 26

A Walk and a Waddle 34

Rock-a-Bye Train 42

Splish! Splash! Splosh!

A snort and a squirt, and a rub-a-dub-dub.

One baby elephant needs a good scrub.

Suck up the water,
spray out a jet

"Come on in, Ellie,
it's time to get wet!"

"I like being dry,
baths are no fun.

I won't jump in, it's nice in the sun."

8

Splish! go the others.

Splash! in the stream.

Splosh! laugh the babies. The mamas all beam.

Ellie stands watching, alone and quite dry.

"The bath looks good! Can I have a try?"

She jumps in the water, gives a loud shout.

Splish! Splash! Splosh!

"I'm NEVER coming out!"

Peekaboo Pup

Woof!
Woof!
Woof!

Puppy wants to play.
Look! There's Bunny, nibbling on a dandelion.

Puppy gets closer,

and closer,

and closer. **Then...**

"Peekaboo, Bunny!"

Puppy wags his tail. **"Ha-ha! Hee-hee!"**
Who could he surprise next?

14

Puppy spots Kitten, snoozing in the sunshine.

Puppy gets closer,

and closer,

and closer. **Then...**

"Peekaboo, Kitten!"

Puppy wags his tail. **"Hee-hee!"**

Puppy is having such a busy morning.

He plays peekaboo on Chicken, and Donkey,
and poor old Mr. Dog!

But then the garden
goes quiet.

Where has everybody gone?

"Peekaboo to YOU, Puppy!"

Little Puppy jumps. Then he giggles and giggles and giggles.

"I love this game," he says. "Let's play every day!"

Can't Catch Me!

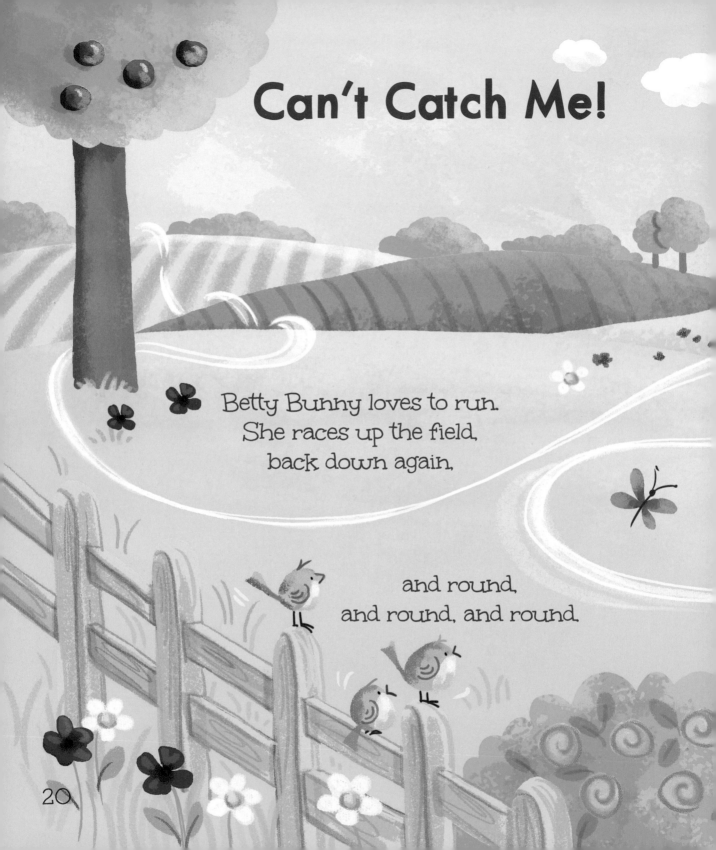

Betty Bunny loves to run.
She races up the field,
back down again,

and round,
and round, and round.

20

"Can't catch me!" she says. "I'm the fastest in this field."

Billy Bird swoops across the sky,

but Betty is faster.

"Can't catch me!" she says.

Sam Squirrel climbs up high,
but Betty is faster.

"Can't catch me!"
she says.

23

Maria Mole digs down deep,
but Betty is faster.

"Can't catch me!" she says.
"Who can I race again?

24

"A bird who flies through the sky,

a squirrel who climbs up **high,**

a mole who digs down **deep,**

or a..."

Uh-oh!

Now Betty's fallen fast asleep!

Tickle Time

Gully is an octopus.

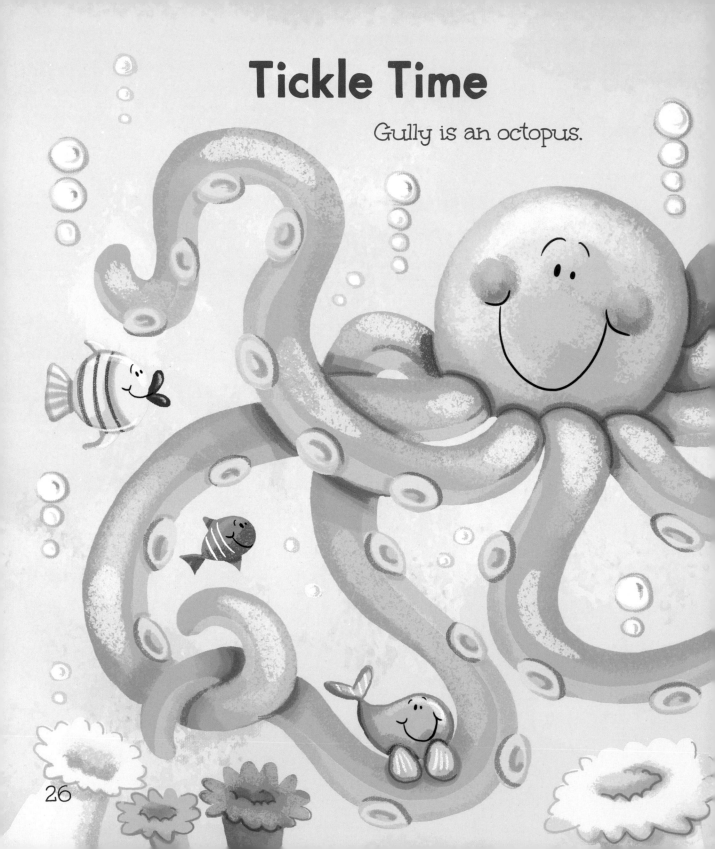

He has a wibbly-wobbly body
and eight flubbery, rubbery tentacles.

Eight is a lot of tentacles.

Gully trips up crabs and ties himself up in knots.

He gets stuck in seaweed and knocks over rocks.

Crash!

Poor Gully.

"Why do I have all these silly tentacles?" he thinks.
"They get me in such a muddle!"
Gully begins to cry.

Gully's daddy is a very big octopus. He has a very big think.

Then he has an idea ...

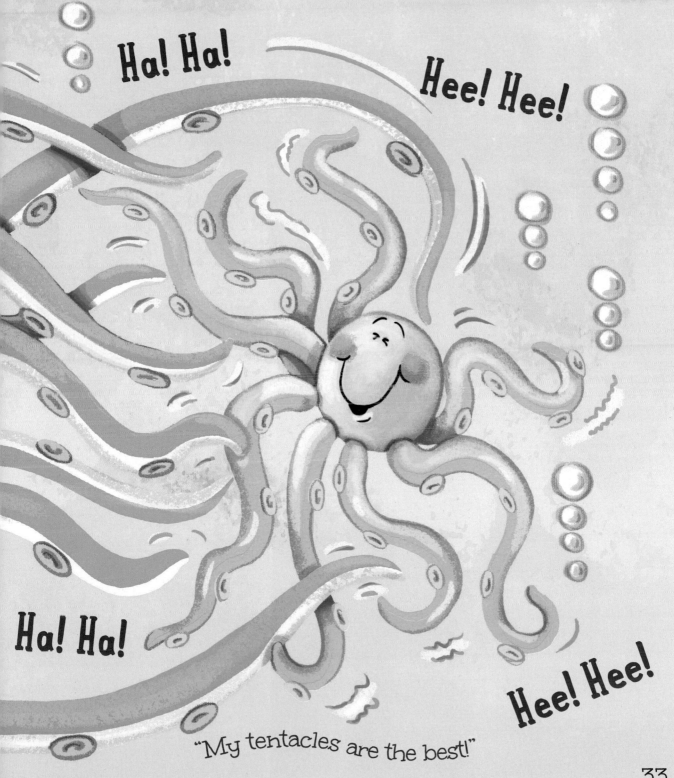

33

A Walk and a Waddle

It was a new day at the zoo.
Penguin was busy exploring.

Penguin walked and Penguin waddled.

But when it was time to go home,
Penguin had a problem.

He was lost.

After a little while, Penguin walked
up to a green, jungly place.

"Is that my
house?" Penguin
asked.

Ooh! Ooh! Aah!

"No!" said the monkeys.
"We live here!"

Penguin waddled up to a brown,
murky swamp.

Snap! Snap! Snap!

"Is that my house?" Penguin asked.
"No!" snapped the crocodiles. "We live here!"

Penguin walked up to a rocky, grassy den.

"Is that my house?" Penguin asked.

Roar! Roar! Roar!

"No!" roared the lions. "We live here!"

Penguin waddled up to a blue, shady pool.

"Is that my house?" Penguin asked.

Snort! Snort! Snort!

"No!" splashed the hippos. "We live here!
But you haven't got far to go..."

39

Penguin turned a corner.

Squawk!

Squawk!

Squawk!

There were penguins EVERYWHERE!
Walking and waddling and swimming in the water.

"Hooray!"
cheered Penguin "I'm home!"

Rock-a-Bye Train

The Rock-a-Bye Train is ready to ride,
All of the passengers tucked up inside.
Rock-a-bye, rock-a-bye, rock.

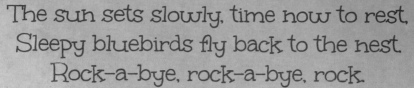

The sun sets slowly, time now to rest,
Sleepy bluebirds fly back to the nest.
Rock-a-bye, rock-a-bye, rock.

Night like a blanket covers the land,
Sing you a lullaby, holding your hand.
Rock-a-bye, rock-a-bye, rock.

Silvery funnel puffing out steam,
Gaze at the stars, it's your time to dream.
Rock-a-bye, rock-a-bye, rock.

45

The Rock-a-Bye Train chugs
under the moon,

Wheels on the rails make a magical tune.
Rock-a-bye, rock-a-bye, rock.

Mamas and papas kiss you goodnight,

Straight on until morning, babies sleep tight.
Rock-a-bye, rock-a-bye, rock.